Noa
and the Little
Elephant

A tale of friendship and survival

*To all creatures great and small
and to all the children of the world
who will look after them*

First published in hardback in Great Britain by HarperCollins *Children's Books* in 2021
HarperCollins *Children's Books* is a division of HarperCollins*Publishers* Ltd,
HarperCollins*Publishers*
1 London Bridge Street
London SE1 9GF

www.harpercollins.co.uk

HarperCollins*Publishers*
1st Floor, Watermarque Building, Ringsend Road
Dublin 4, Ireland

1

Text and illustrations copyright © Michael Foreman 2021

Hardback ISBN: 978-00-0-841327-9
Paperback ISBN: 978-00-0-841328-6

Michael Foreman asserts the moral right to be identified as
the author and illustrator of this work.

Printed and bound by RR Donnelley APS in China.

Noa
and the Little
Elephant

A tale of friendship and survival

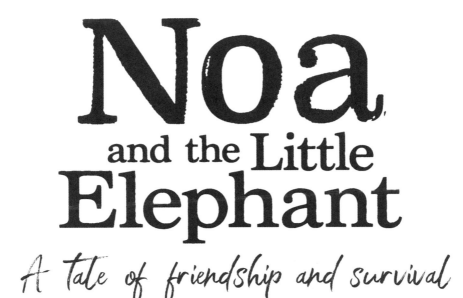

MICHAEL FOREMAN

HarperCollins *Children's Books*

Foreword
Julius Obwona, Ranger
UGANDA WILDLIFE AUTHORITY

I grew up living next to Murchison Falls National Park in Uganda. My mother reminds me of how long I took to be able to say the words "elephant" and "giraffe", but how I was always in awe of these animals.

Walking to collect water or helping on the farm, I saw elephants, antelopes, birds and colourful insects. Wildlife has always been part of my life – I could easily be Noa!

As a young man, my innocent world began to change. Poaching brought elephant numbers down from 16,000 to just a few hundred, and my peaceful savanna and beautiful streams and rivers turned red. My childhood dreams were broken; my heart was broken.

My purpose in life became to protect the voiceless. I needed to help my rumbling elephant friends, leaping antelopes, roaring lions and pretty giraffes.

I made my promise.

For the past twenty years I have worked for the Uganda Wildlife Authority as a ranger and I am now in charge of protecting all wildlife in Murchison Falls. I live a life, as others do across Africa, as the trusted shadow of the elephants and other animals.

On patrol I often find myself quietly chatting to them. "Good morning, Mrs Elephant. Your babies are looking so healthy – enjoy your day!" And then I laugh at myself, hoping nobody saw me doing it!

We now have nearly 3,000 elephants, and our giraffes have increased from 400 to 2,000. We are doing our best – sometimes without socks and boots – but we won't stop. They need us every day.

We made our promise.

Africa's rangers, like me, dream of the day you will visit and we can introduce you to the paradise we live in. Then you will be able to say hi to Mrs Elephant and her friends too!

Until then, we promise to do our best to ensure the wildlife is protected and safe.

Noa loved being on the river.
He went fishing every day after
school in his little boat that his father
had built for his birthday.

He was so proud to take fish home
for the family supper.

He liked to watch all the amazing animals
attracted to the cool waters of the great river:
wading birds, stripy zebras and the tall
giraffes that had to spread their long legs
wide to drink.

Most of all, Noa loved to watch the mother elephant and her baby.

Each day, they came to wallow in the cool river. Noa laughed every time the mother hosed the baby with her trunk and the baby squirted her back.

The elephants got used to seeing Noa and,
sometimes, he would join in their water games.

One day, the elephants did not come to the river. Noa waited in the shade of the banyan tree, fishing, but still the elephants did not come.

"If they won't come to me, I will go to them," decided Noa.

He followed the well-worn elephant tracks
from the river through the dark jungle.

Unseen creatures rushed and rustled in the
undergrowth, and monkeys swung in trees above
his head. But there was no sign of the elephants.

Then, as he came out into open country on the far side of the jungle, Noa saw the mother elephant lying down and her baby gently bumping her with his head.

A strange new game, thought Noa.

When he got closer, however, he saw this was no game. The baby was trying to wake his mother, but Noa could see that the great elephant would never wake up.

She was not moving and her wonderful white tusks had been cut off.

At first the baby elephant was frightened when he saw Noa, but then he recognised his riverbank friend and slowly walked towards him, swinging his trunk and sadly shaking his head from side to side.

Noa stroked his ear and the baby elephant gently wrapped his trunk round him. They hugged each other.

"Come home with me, my friend," Noa said. "I will look after you."

Together they walked slowly through the jungle to Noa's home at the edge of the village.

Noa's mum and little sister, Eva, were amazed when he arrived home with the young elephant, but quickly made the little orphan welcome with a bucket of goat's milk.

"Thin the milk with a little water," said Dad, who knew a lot about elephants. "It will be too rich for him otherwise, and might make him sick."

Dad told Noa about the hunters who shot elephants with guns and poison arrows to steal their valuable tusks.

"That's awful," cried Noa. "So cruel. It should be stopped!"

"We are trying to stop it," said Dad. "The villagers have formed a group to try to protect the elephants."

"If he's going to be one of the family, we must give him a name," said Mum.

"Tembo," said Eva. "Tembo the elephant."

In the next days and weeks, the little
elephant became not just part of the family,
but part of village life.

He helped carry water from the well, and
wood from the forest.

Sometimes he followed Noa to school
and joined in the playground games.

He was sad but happy at the same time
to be playing with his new friend, Noa.

One night, there was a tremendous storm.
It was the beginning of the rainy season and all
night long thunder boomed and lightning flashed.

The next morning, the river was rushing and roaring
and bursting over the banks. Noa ran to make sure
that his boat was safe from the floodwater.

As he tried to pull the boat higher up the bank, he was caught by a huge swoosh of water. The boat, and Noa, were swept into the raging river. He tried to stay afloat, but the wild, muddy river roared, and the churning current kept dragging him under.

Then he felt something solid under his feet.
It seemed to bump him towards the bank, and
he grabbed at an overhanging branch and
hung on.

He hooked his legs over the branch and dragged
himself into the safety of the tree.

Suddenly Tembo emerged from the river below him.
He had been the "something solid" beneath Noa's feet.

"Thank you, Tembo," cried Noa. "Thank you for
saving me!"

Tembo waved his trunk and helped Noa
safely down from the tree.

Together, the two friends made their way home.
A rainbow appeared over the village.

"When I'm older," said Noa, stroking Tembo's trunk, "I will join my dad and the other villagers to make sure that no more elephants are shot. You are my brother. We are all one family living under the same sky and sharing the same world."

About Tusk

Tusk is a charity set up in 1990 to help to protect African wildlife, including the African elephant, black rhino and mountain gorilla. We help local organisations to make an even greater difference, and support more than sixty field projects in more than twenty African countries. We not only work to protect wildlife, but also help to reduce poverty through sustainable development. HRH the Duke of Cambridge became the charity's Royal Patron in 2005 and has been a proactive supporter ever since.

To support our work and find out more visit www.tusk.org.